Whatever Happened, Happened for good

Written by Emmet Fox

Illustrated by Moch. Fajar Shobaru

First published 2022 by Chenesis Publishing, London, UK

Text copyright Emmet Fox 2022

Illustrations copyright Emmet Fox 2022

Once upon a time in a very busy city lived Bert and Tom. They were best of friends.

Bert was very wise. He often used to say, "Try not to be sad" and "Whatever happens, happens for good."

One day Bert and Tom were out playing with their scooters. They loved to play on scooters and went out everywhere with them.

They went up hills. They went down hills. They even did tricks on them.

6

7

One day, Tom fell off his scooter and landed hard on the ground. Tom yelped while holding his leg. He was in a lot of pain. He cut his leg and had a big bruise.

Bert quickly comforted Tom, "Try not to be sad. Whatever happens, happens for good."

8

Tom got very angry. He shouted, "My leg is hurting, there is a bruise and a cut, and you are saying that it has happened for good. What is good?"

Tom told Bert to go away and not come back again. They would not be going out with their scooters together anymore.

Bert was not sad by this and as he left, he said, "Whatever happens, happens for good."

Tom was surprised to hear this.

He thought that Bert was strange and that they were no longer going to be friends.

One month passed since the incident.

One day Tom went out scooting on his own. He went up the hills and down the hills. He was in the fields and saw in a distant a flashing bright light.

It was an amazing colour and he wanted to see what it was. He scooted fast towards it. Little did he know, it was a spaceship from a distant planet.

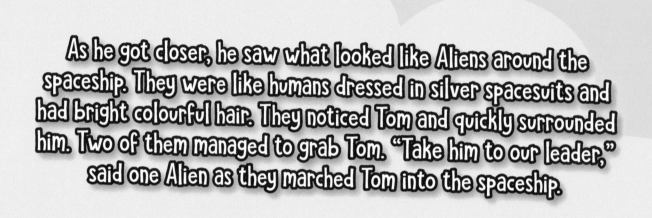

As he got closer, he saw what looked like Aliens around the spaceship. They were like humans dressed in silver spacesuits and had bright colourful hair. They noticed Tom and quickly surrounded him. Two of them managed to grab Tom. "Take him to our leader," said one Alien as they marched Tom into the spaceship.

15

The leader sat in a big red leather chair.

He looked at Tom and said, "Our mission is to take a human to our planet to show everyone what they look like." Tom pleaded with the leader to let him go, but the leader did not want to listen.

The Aliens in the spaceship started to dance to music and wave their arms in the air. Two of them dragged Tom towards a small glass room.

Just as they were about to place Tom into the room, the leader shouted, "Stop! What is that on his leg?"

The leader saw that Tom had a mark and a scab on his leg.

Tom replied that he had hurt himself while riding his scooter.

The leader ordered the music and dancing to stop. They would not be taking Tom. They wanted a human without any marks, as the people on his planet will not be happy.

19

They took Tom out of the spaceship and left him in the field with his scooter.

Soon the spaceship lifted and flew fast away into the sky.

Tom got onto his scooter and quickly scooted off through the fields back to his home.

After dinner, Tom thought about how if he had not fallen and hurt himself, the Aliens would have put him in a glass box and taken him away to their planet.

He realised Bert was right, "Whatever happened, happened for good."

Tom called Bert and told him he was sorry and wanted to be friends again.

When they both met, Tom said that he understood what Bert meant when he said that "Whatever happened, happened for good." But he asked Bert, "What good happened to you?" when he told him to go away.

Bert smiled and said, "You and I are best friends and we always go scooting together. Had you not told me to go away that day and not be your friend, I would have been with you when you met the Aliens. They left you after seeing the marks on your leg, but I did not have any marks and had I been with you they would have put me in the glass box and taken me to their planet. That's why it was good I was not with you that day. It saved your life and saved my life. That's why I always say, try and not be sad, and that whatever happens, happens for good."

They both smiled and got on their scooters and scooted off.

The End.

26

Lightning Source UK Ltd.
Milton Keynes UK
UKHW050459080223
416583UK00003B/59